The Go-kart

Series created by Roderick Hunt and Alex Brychta

Written by Roderick Hunt
Illustrated by Alex Brychta

BEFORE READING

Talk together

- Read the title together. Use the picture to talk about go-karts.
- Ask your child whether they would like to have a go on this go-kart.
- Look through the book and talk about the pictures.

About the words in this book

- Your child should be able to sound out and blend some words, which may include:

a Dad had it Mum

- Some words may be more challenging. Encourage or model blending, then read the words below to your child if necessary.

they made go-kart
wanted pushed pulled
stop said away
swing oh

DURING READING

Enjoy the story together. If your child needs support to read the words:

- Ask your child to point from left to right under each word whilst reading.
- Model how to sound out and blend new words if necessary.
- If a word is still too tricky, simply say the whole word for your child.
- Use the pictures to talk about the story and learn the meaning of new words.

See the inside back cover for more ideas.

Dad made a go-kart.

Biff wanted the go-kart.

Chip wanted the go-kart.

Biff wanted a go.

Chip wanted a go.

Biff pushed.

Chip pulled.

They had a fight.

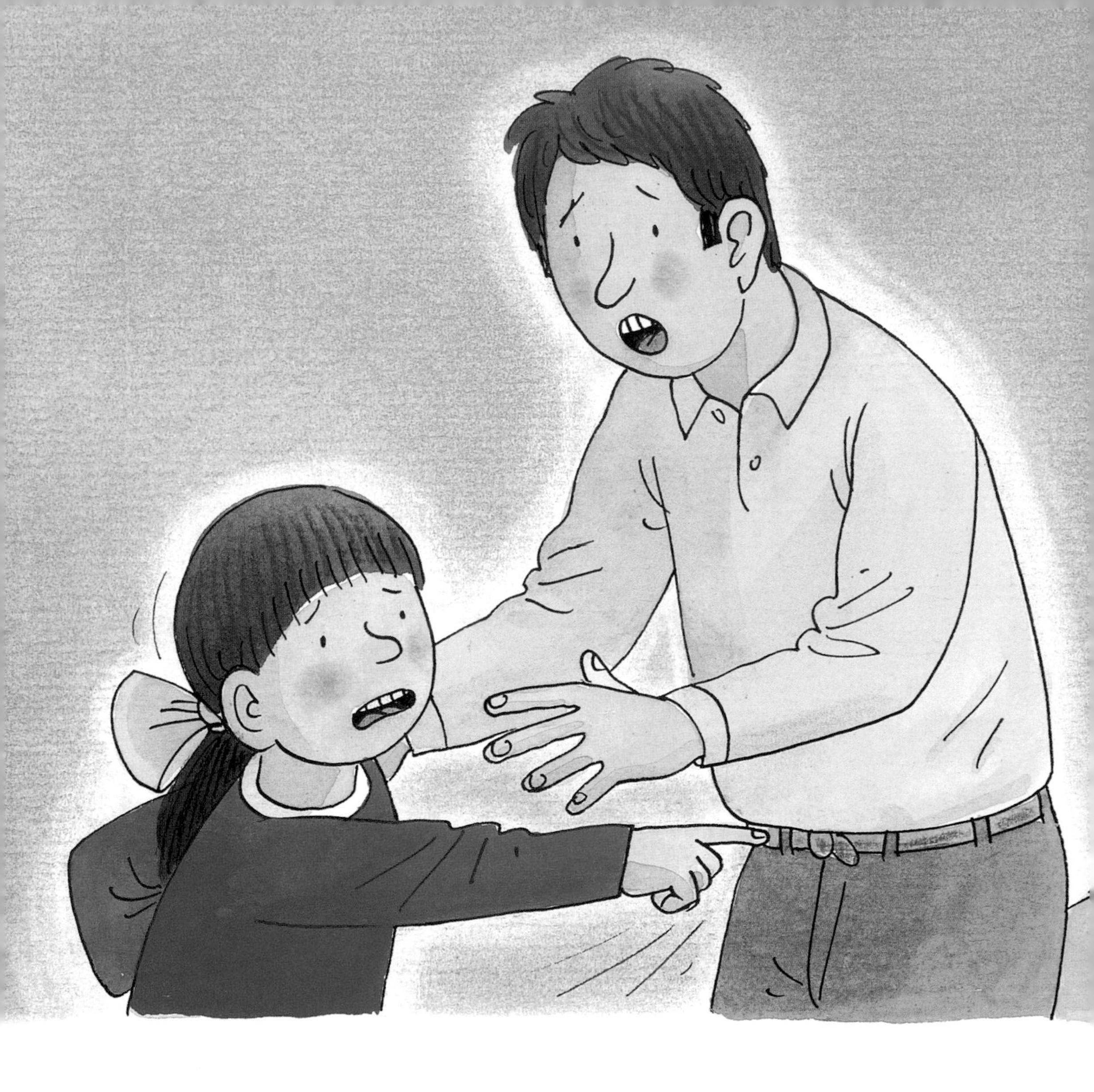

“Stop it,” said Dad.

“Stop it,” said Mum.

Dad put the go-kart away.

They made a swing.

GARDEN SWING
INSTRUCTIONS

Oh no!